Gone

The Missing Years of Bjorn Esterday

Book 08

Lab

2031-2032

Wynter Sommers

GONE: The Missing Years of Bjorn Esterday

USA Copyright © 2015 GJ dePillis
© TXu002023789 and TXu002010532 / 2016

Library of Congress Control Number: 2021936597

Published by Pure Force Enterprises, Inc.
California, USA
Since 2002

INGRAM

INGRAM® Distribution

ISBN-13: 978-1-7184-0037-5
ISBN-10: 1-7184-0037-3

DEDICATION

To those who feel strongly about truth, justice, and the integrity of America; your honorable actions make us proud.

To those who wonder if their daily choices matter; your small decisions impact generations to come.

To those everyday people who don't think they have what it takes; your perseverance and strive for the extraordinary, makes the impossible a reality.

To those who have failed; know you will make it and tomorrow will be better.

Your dreams today become our future tomorrow.
Thank you for everything you do.

Bjorn Esterday
Was Not Born Yesterday
Series

Firebrand (15 Volumes+Conversation Station Book)
Edges (9 Stories +Conversation Station Book)
Gone (24 Stories + Conversation Station Book +
Longfellow Journal for 26 books in Gone set)

Bjorn EDGES Series
EDGES Book 1-Swift Encounter
EDGES Book 2-Rousing Attack
EDGES Book 3-One Foot Under
EDGES Book 4-Earthshake
EDGES Book 5-Broken String
EDGES Book 6-Key Witness
EDGES Book 7-Who is She?
EDGES Book 8-Vanish
EDGES Book 9-Chase or Die

Bjorn Series Alternate Reading Plan

1st	Edges Book 1		25th	Gone Book 11
2nd	Edges Book 2		26th	Firebrand Vol 10
3rd	Gone Book 1		27th	Gone Book 12
4th	Firebrand Vol 1		28th	Gone Book 13
5th	Edges Book 3		29th	Firebrand Vol 11
6th	Firebrand Vol 2		30th	Gone Book 14
7th	Gone Book 2		31st	Gone Book 15
8th	Gone Book 3		32nd	Firebrand Vol 12
9th	Firebrand Vol 3		33rd	Gone Book 16
10th	Gone Book 4		34th	Gone Book 17
11th	Firebrand Vol 4		35th	Firebrand Vol 13
12th	Gone Book 5		36th	Gone Book 18
13th	Gone Book 6		37th	Gone Book 19
14th	Gone Book 25- *Longfellow's Journal*		38th	Edges Book 5
			39th	Edges Book 6
15th	Edges Book 4		40th	Gone Book 20
16th	Firebrand Vol 5		41st	Gone Book 21
17th	Gone Book 7		42nd	Edges Book 7
18th	Firebrand Vol 6		43rd	Gone Book 22
19th	Gone Book 8		44th	Firebrand Vol 14
20th	Firebrand Vol 7		45th	Firebrand Vol15 (End)
21st	Gone Book 9		46th	Edges Book 8
22nd	Firebrand Vol 8		47th	Edges Book 9(End)
23rd	Gone Book 10		48th	Gone Book 23
24th	Firebrand Vol 9		49th	Gone Book 24(End)

ACKNOWLEDGMENTS

We acknowledge those who honorably build peace. We acknowledge all the selfless talent which contributed to creating meaningful tokens of consideration and sharing. We acknowledge that every person has a daily choice of right or wrong... and we thank you for choosing the right, good, honorable path filled with integrity because that is the difficult and brave path. Small choices today become lasting monuments of loving hope tomorrow.

HOW TO INTERPRET THE CHAPTER TITLES

How to read this book: The title has two numbers. The number on the left is the chapter order in this book. The number on the right of "chapter" is the consecutive continuous chapter in the entire series. The number in parentheses is the year and the rest is a chapter title, sometimes sharing which location the chapter takes place.

*For example, below is a chapter which appears in GONE Book #03. It is chapter 6, but GONE continuous saga chapter **13**. The action takes place in the year 2030 in the location of Brio in the Gardens. The* year is in parenthesis.

6 CHAPTER *13*: (2030) BRIO: GARDENS

CONTENTS

Settings

Locations

- **AromaX**: City of fragrance & fashion

- **Courtly City**: City of solar & other technical products. Bjorn Esterday and Sarah Paradise live here.

- **Brio**: Underwater village managed by Zor who works with Watson, the motivational speaker.

Characters

- **Dr. Lou Pole Linden**: Research assistant to Otto Mattick in the AromaX labs

- **Georgia Peach**: Fellow-teacher at Sarah Paradise's school.

- **Sarah Paradise**: Teacher. She met Bjorn Esterday in the EDGES series

- **Watson**: Charismatic motivational speaker

- **Lou Pole Linden**: Works in the AromaX labs

- **Tres**: Works with Watson

- **Female1**: Test Subject in the AromaX lab run by Dr. Linden and funded by the Twins

- **Male1:** Test Subject in the AromaX lab run by Dr. Linden and funded by the Twins

- **Male2:** Test Subject in the AromaX lab, but first to undergo Dr. Linden's NanoNevel procedure

0 PREFACE

Innovation.

What is the price of being innovative? On what will we experiment? How much will we risk to obtain our envisioned goal? If achieved, would the expense be worth it? Once discovered, how do we get others to adopt it and make the invention mainstream?

Should we keep credit for ourselves or share it openly with the world anonymously?

If we meant it for good, but a powerful force used it for evil...would we comply with the nefarious governings of our misused invention, or would we call upon our integrity and put a stop to it? If you can sell your integrity at the right price, what will you do when you encounter another individual who cannot be bribed?

Last time, in the year 2031, we saw Bjorn encounter dogs on the island, but when he tries to get his bearings he wakes up in a house, in a bed...something he has not experienced in ages.

It is clear, however, that Longfellow, wants Bjorn gone as soon as possible. Realizing how far away he is from Courtly City, and his lack of communications, Bjorn tries desperately to make the best of the situation.

In the year 2032, we see that Otto Mattick and Topliner have made arrangements to live and work at the theater in Rough-N-Ready. It is in this remote outpost town that Topliner encounters Slash and Percy Snatcher of the AnCors, unaware that this group has already negatively impacted his family... and may be responsible for the disappearance of his mother. Or is Topliner not so naïve, and is really exacting his own plans?

Back in 2031, at the Linden Lab in AromaX, Lou Pole Linden orders something to achieve his vision of creating the ultimate MagSol....

1 CHAPTER 37: (2031) AROMAX: LAB: LOU POLE LINDEN GETS A CRATE, OPENS IT, MAKES A LIST

A driverless flatbed robotic delivery vehicle eased through the entrance of Dr. Lou Pole Linden's lab in AromaX. The sound of hydraulic lifts angled the truck bed until a large crate slipped off and dropped onto the floor. Lou Pole Linden held his breath. His package had arrived.

The flatbed reversed out of the room without turning around. Lou Pole Linden waited, frozen in place until he heard the motor of the delivery vehicle leave the grounds.

Then, he tip-toed to the crate, picked up the opening device, and inhaled slowly. Having the crate fully opened, Lou Pole Linden smiled at the contents.

Out tumbled three very homeless, dirty looking people. Alive. Two men. One woman.

Inside was a note, which Lou Pole Linden skimmed in a sing-songy tone as he stepped away from the three unconscious bodies to a window to get some fresh air,

"As requested, their families were killed during the transfer to the Twins so nobody will miss them. Good luck."

He nodded, then began unceremoniously dragging the three unconscious people toward his surgery. After a brief effort, he became tired and sat down to fix himself a cup of tea, wondering how to lift his new bodies onto each prepared operating table.

While the heavy deep breathing of the

three homeless souls started to annoy Lou Pole Linden, he walked to his computer and turned on some music to drown out their noise.

"Of course!" he exclaimed as the thought struck him, "I'll wait for them to wake up, then they can put themselves where I want them." Lou smiled satisfied that he was solving problems left and right.

He scooted to where Otto Mattick had last left some notes, and mumbled as he looked through them.

"Formula, procedures, materials," Lou Pole Linden was getting frustrated as he muttered, "Carbon aerogel epoxy polymer composite can act as a shield against hot and cold... Fullerene nanostructures in hydrogenated amorphous carbon film... Aggregated diamonds have an isothermal bulk modulus of 491 gigapascals, which is stronger than carbon diamonds... I wonder if that is too opaque for a visor... or Lexan? Oh! Here it is!

Transparent Alumina. Stronger than steel and one can see right through it."

He glanced over his shoulder. Annoyance crossed his face. His three Guinea-pig-humans still had not awakened.

Shaking his head, he went to the three homeless test subjects and looked down at them.

"Ha! Skipper Courtly's Soldier Police uniforms are going to look like toddler onesies compared to what I'm going to make you wear!"

None of the test subjects moved.

2 CHAPTER 38: (2031) AROMAX: LAB: LOU POLE LINDEN EXPLAINS TO THE HOMELESS TEST SUBJECTS

Fully awake, each of Dr. Lou Pole Linden's three homeless test subjects, now wearing hospital smocks, sat on the edge of their assigned cots.

Lou Pole Linden, in his warehouse makeshift hospital room, smoothed his moustache as he positioned himself in front of them to announce,

"You three have been hand selected to… well, be part of the new power grid."

"Power grid?" the woman said.

"Yes. I am going to make you more powerful," Lou Pole Linden explained.

One of the homeless men said, "At the shelter, we were told that if we agreed to help out in a lab, we'd get free meals and a bed to sleep in."

Lou Pole Linden reached out and tapped an intravenous bag tied to a pole with a long tube extending from it and said, "And indeed the person who enlisted your valuable services told the truth. You shall be fed nutrients from here, and you will have a nice bed to sleep in. Here." Lou pole Linden tapped the hospital cot where the man sat.

The woman asked, as she looked around, "Sir? He made it sound more... well... cozy than this place."

The other man spoke up. "We were all at the shelter, Dr. Linden," he started, but was interrupted.

"I don't care about any of that, my friend," Lou Pole Linden smiled.

"But I wish you would care," the man continued. "You see we were once respectable people. I had a job. She had a job. He had a job. I worked construction."

The woman said, "I was an accountant at a bank." The other man said, "I used to be an architect."

The first man continued, "And, Dr. Linden, all our families were executed during the Twin takeover."

The woman interrupted, "Well, all our families were driven to survive one disaster or another."

Lou Pole Linden nodded, "We have all had to accept that the plague opened the door for the Twins to take over, however, now we all do our part to support the Twins empire."

The woman scoffed, "I would never say

anything against the Twins. I would never accuse them of obtaining power by spreading chaos. I would never tell anybody that the Twins gathered more and more power with shadow diplomats."

"Shadow diplomat?"

Nodding, the woman shrugged, "I do not have a head for such things. I made that term up. I think the shadow comes from working in the dark or having illicit financial streams where the credits cannot be traced to a source. Or having tax-havens in unethical areas where the credits cannot be touched to contribute to the functioning of AromaX society, like road maintenance or affordable housing."

"If they are in the shadows, they are inconsequential." Linden smirked.

"I agree," The woman nodded, "The Twins are wise and all knowing. I would never suggest that they gained control through corporate wrongdoing, bribing or blackmailing corporate-government officials, senseless murders, or malicious propaganda leading the masses to believe the Twins would care for the people instead of funneling off all the resources for themselves. Never. I support you, Dr. Linden. I recognize the Twins are in power and punish any person who has a negative opinion of them... I am just a woman without an opinion saying only nice things about the Twins." She sighed and muttered to herself, "....trying to forget the employed life I used to have."

"That's a good girl. Comply with the mandates," Dr. Linden advised, "They do reward loyalty ....if they feel like it."

The man protested, "But, Dr. Linden....Why help the regime which only gained power by force and stealing. If we were permitted to have our elections and only presented with the evidence-based, we would never have voted for for the Twins to come to power."

The woman glared at the man with a warning, "You must only say the Twins are good, else you risk instant death for uttering negative sentiments against the Twins."

The man fell silent.

The man retorted, "I only said that about the Twins because I believe Dr. Linden would be a better supreme overlord of AromaX. He stands before us as a man to admire...."

They nodded in agreement and smiled at Dr. Linden.

Dr. Linden smiled, "Look at where we are. I am the one making the rules here. You are safe to think that I would be a better leader than the Twins. You may continue this conversation. Why do you dislike the regime of the Twins?"

After hesitating a moment, the man continued, "When the Twins gained power, my family was told donating the land would result in riches, yet they just evicted us from our land, stole my family's property which had been ours for generations. We saw no reward for cooperating with them. We also got the same treatment as those who voiced protests. What we said did not matter. The Twins took our goods and claimed it as theirs. No longer could a citizen save up for years to buy a home. The masses were turned out into the streets to live rough. Some died trying to protect their property. Only the chosen ones, like you Dr. Linden, were given what was once our goods as a reward for your loyalty to the Twins." He smiled, "And now here we are, at your disposal, for your experiments."

The woman interjected, "If the people had listened to the medical professionals... the wise ones like Dr. Linden, who would make a far better leader... I mean..."

"Go on," Dr. Lou Pole Linden urged with a satisfied smile.

She continued, "When the plague came,

the people listened to the propaganda the Twins put out there. So many people did not get vaccinated. Many people did not even use that invented Mailable Inspector Collector disposable detector."

Gasping Dr. Linden leaned in, "I recall the debates over ID11,077,436. AromaX wanted to make *Mailable Inspector Collectors* here and export to Courtly City and the other corporate cities to identify the plague early and then isolate the infected to give them early treatments."

The woman nodded, "So, if you had actually used that invention, Dr. Linden, you would have been viewed by the people as a hero, and you would be in power instead of the Twins."

Thinking to himself, Dr. Linden agreed with a shrug, "But not using the Mailable Inspector Collector is our decision from the past. We now have our new mighty leaders. I have my orders. And now I have you. I thank you all for helping me use my brilliant mind to prove my own invention."

I was told I'd be helping you out in a lab. I could clean. I could take notes... I'm willing to do that in exchange for food and shelter. No extra pay, but I'm not sure about having you do experiments on... well, at least me..."

"Me too," the woman agreed.

"I second that," the other man concurred.

Scoffing, Dr. Linden stiffened, "You wish to be my janitor when I offer to give you strength as you have never had before?"

The woman inquired, "You mean way back when we used to be able to vote and have strength as a united people who wanted the best for our communities?"

Gradually becoming red in the face with frustration, Dr. Linden seethed , "No. I offer to make you stronger!"

The man asked, "So we can help you

build your empire better than the Twins?"

Shaking his head with disbelief that this tiny, homeless audience was not understanding, Dr. Linden laboriously explained slowly, "I do not want an empire. That would mean aggregating and unifying states. What an administrative headache. No... I've learned real power is conquering with violence and buying loyalty with wealth."

The man nodded, "I do not think they teach that in the old management schools. Some may consider that a path to encouraging corruption..."

The woman cut him off, realizing that the man's comment might anger Dr. Linden. Hurriedly she interjected, "That Mailable Inspector Collector device was a good idea. The making of it, producing it, would have created an income stream for AromaX even though it was not directly linked to the beauty or fashion sectors... It would have allowed crowds to gather safely. Maybe we could help you invent something else like that?"

Lou Pole Linden exhaled and hung his head, "Why save ungrateful people with a Mailable Inspector Collector?   The people would not have appreciated it. As you know, those who got early medical treatment, who actually got vaccinated, were in the minority. So the virus incubated and mutated in the bodies of all the people refusing to be vaccinated..."

The man nodded and echoed, "Each wave of mutated variants opened the door wider for the Twins to come in with any promise to solve our plague problem, and then to seize power... and destroy our goods on a whim..."

Dr. Linden agreed, "Now you understand. The Twins put people like you, who are obviously not blindly loyal to them, on the streets... and you survived."

"So why us?" The other man asked.

Linden explained, "I need you because after all the plagues, after destroying your goods, after everything you have endured, you are like a wind-battered tree where the grain has been refined by the torments of the environment. If, after all the hardships the Twin's rule created for you, and you have endured, then you are strong enough to withstand my experiments. And know this, my pets, my future MagSol pets, you will always have a home with me."

One man echoed, "Pets?"

Becoming annoyed, Lou Pole Linden looked up at the ceiling, then down at his feet. He took a deep breath and said, "Listen. I'm going to make you stronger and..."

The woman interrupted, "I'd really appreciate a hot meal... one, I can chew, then swallow... Instead of trying to push my face into a bag of intravenous nutrients..."

She started to scoot off the cot and

walk directly to the pile where her clothes had been dropped in a crumpled heap.

Lou Pole Linden quickly stepped in her way and said softly, "I need you. You are the most important one of the three. Please stay and keep me company…"

"Why am I any more special than those two?" she asked.

"You are special, my dear," Dr. Lou Pole Linden explained to the homeless woman, "because if the experiment is successful, instead of starting from scratch and lining up artificial muscles with your…homegrown muscles, your DNA should have changed and that means…"

He stopped talking.

"Hey!" she said as she took a step back from him. "What are you saying? I'm homeless, not stupid." She looked at the two men and asked, "Do you realize what the doctor is saying?"

The men shook their heads.

The homeless woman replied, "He's saying that if the experiment takes and we all get stronger, I'm supposed to breed with you two characters to make MagSol babies." She quickly turned back to the doctor and announced, "This gutter trash understands what you're saying, Doc."

Lou Pole Linden shook his head. "You don't understand. You don't have to breed with both of them, just the one who survives."

"Who survives?" both men said in unison.

Lou Pole Linden held both his hands up and said, "Fine! My goodness! I get it! You don't understand science, so you fear it. I was hoping to use logic to help you understand the honor I am about to bestow upon you, but…"

The woman retorted, "Hey! I know what 'science' is, mister, and this ain't it!"

Lou Pole Linden shrugged, reached into his pocket, extracted a hand-held tranquilizer gun, and shot all three.

They collapsed within a few seconds of getting hit.

Once contributing citizens with jobs, homes and names… these three were now subject to Dr. Linden's unknown experiments.

3 CHAPTER 39: (2031) AROMAX: LAB: LOU POLE LINDEN BEGINS THE MOLD FOR THE FIRST OF THREE EXOSKELETONS

Lou Pole Linden, wearing a freshly cleaned smock, was in another part of the warehouse.

He had his hair in a shower cap, and a special covering just for his moustache.

With long plastic gloves, which went up to his elbows, he manipulated the materials in front of him.

Occasionally he would stop and listen

to the shouts of his chained up test subjects down the hall.

He smirked.

"Ah, the homeless," he said, "never eat a meal nourishing enough to give them the strength to break out of chains. Besides, how could they possibly appreciate I'm about to give them strength beyond their wildest dreams?"

His three human subjects were obviously trying to pull on the chains and free themselves, but to no avail.

Lou Pole Linden looked down at his list as if it were a cooking recipe and read aloud, "Lay Kevlar net against the fullerene carbon- hydrogen nano-structures amorphous diamond film until still pliable. Then shape against desired mold." He shook his head, "Why can't there be an online instructional video showing how to do this?" he spat shaking his head at yet another assumption that scientists do not require clear recipe instructions for assembly.

Frustrated over not having clear repeatable instructions to follow, he clenched his jaw and continued.

He carefully positioned the material and then gingerly stepped away to another work station where there was a motorcycle helmet. He popped off the visor to examine the curve of the lens. He then coated it and muttered, "Now to see if I can use this as a mold for the Aluminum Oxynitride so we can have visors of transparent alumina."

He busied himself, carefully measuring, sculpting, molding, and timing each step.

Lou Pole Linden heard something slam noisily to the floor in the room where the three homeless test subjects had been stored.

Quickly peeling off his gloves, shower cap, and mustache covering, Dr. Linden raced out of his work room and down the hall toward the noise, chanting to himself, "I've got to get the NanoNevel working to start the infusion."

4 CHAPTER 40: (2031) AROMAX: LAB: LINDEN SCOLDS HIS CHILDISH GUESTS

Reaching for his tranquilizer gun, again, Dr. Lou Pole Linden shook his head as he realized he was running out of actual tranquilizer cartridges.

Then, standing there in the hallway of his makes-shift hospital experimental lab, he heard a timer ding from the workroom.

The exoskeleton armor he was building back in the work room down the hall was ready for the next step of the procedure. But in front of him, in the room where his homeless test subjects were held, he heard another crash.

Even without having time to reload his tranquilizers, he raced toward the sound of the commotion. When he opened the door, he saw that one of the homeless males had taken the IV pole and used it to smash up whatever it could reach.

They stopped when they saw Dr. Linden enter the room.

"You ingrates!" Dr. Linden exclaimed. "I feed you..."

Linden set the IV pole upright again and picked up the intravenous bag, which had fallen to the floor, as he continued, "I clothe you..." he indicated the hospital gowns they wore, "I give you beds to sleep in," he straighten up the cots, which were now askew, one turned on its side.

Each bed had displayed a hand written

sign. The signs were Male1, Male2 and Female1. He looked around the floor and found the missing sign, which read Female1 and attached it back onto the foot of the cot to which the woman was chained.

Dr. Linden put both his hands on his hips and scolded, "Even though I'm about to make you very strong..."

He looked each one in the eyes.

"Now, I am very disappointed in your dreadful behavior. If you act like children, I will treat you as children."

The woman spat, "We were homeless before we came here, but we were free and not chained!" She took a deep breath, "What psychopath would chain up a child to teach them manners? You are not treating us like children. You are treating us like prisoners."

Male1 asked softly, "You want to hear how much we appreciate what you've done for us, don't you?"

Dr. Linden smiled, nodding, and said, "That's exactly it. I'm going through a lot of effort, here and don't feel very appreciated."

Male2 asked, "If we thank you for everything, Dr. Linden, will you let us go?"

5 CHAPTER 41: (2031) AROMAX: LAB: LINDEN PROPOSES THE NANONEVEL

Dr. Linden gave a disapproving sigh as he observed these three test subjects.

Lou Pole Linden knew he couldn't get others. He knew the Twins were expecting results. If he didn't at least try to come up with something, Dr. Lou Pole Linden would be the next casualty of the Twins' Transfer of Power.

"I wish you could see how important this is," Dr. Linden pleaded. "Let me help you understand. It will give you a new occupation. A new life. I explained the whole process of artificial muscle infusion with the NanoNevel to you earlier."

The three, Female1, Male1 and Male2 all looked at each other, speechless. They almost felt sorry for their captor.

"You don't need three test subjects," Female1 said. "I think your sponsors, the Twins, just want to see some return on their investment in your lab. So, we know you are developing an exoskeleton suit of armor. Why not just focus on perfecting that? Maybe we can even help you. So you won't need to waste any more time on trying out your artificial muscle fibers?"

Male1 chimed in, "We were brought here because we thought you needed an assistant, not a test subject. So, if you employ us... for food and shelter as we originally agreed, then we can still be your assistants and help develop your armor."

Male2 added, "Right. Construction, architecture, and understanding about costs to replicate. We got it all here."

"Guys," Dr. Linden said as he twirled his mustache, "See? I like it when we talk like this. I feel part of the team, now. Not some," he rolled his hands and eyes in unison, "some alpha leader. Lovely. We are all friends, right?"

The three, still chained to their cots which were anchored to the wall, nodded fervently and offered phrases like, "Since childhood", "Best of friends", and "You got it, buddy."

Smiling brightly, Dr. Linden replied, "Now the twins are expecting MagSols." He shrugged, "So, I think it's time to test out the NanoNevel, don't you?"

Dr. Linden extracted the tranquilizer gun from his pocket and shot Male2, who slowly sank to the floor unconscious.

Female1 shouted at Dr. Linden, "Why do you keep knocking us out!"

Dr. Linden replied, "Because you wouldn't let me get close enough to inject you properly."

Male1 asked, "So, you don't want us as assistants for your armor development?"

Dr. Linden put his tranquilizer gun back in his pocket and grabbed the ankles of Male2, now unconscious on the ground.

To Male1, Dr. Linden said, "Well, assistant Male1, help me get Male2 into surgery and onto the operating table."

Male1 looked at Female1. She stared back.

"Dr. Linden, are you going to unchain me so I can help you lift him up?" Male1 asked.

"No! Your chain has enough slack. You can reach him," Dr. Lou Pol Linden advised.

Male1 feigned helplessness, unable to

even shift Male2.

Dr. Linden struggled under the weight, but eventually lifted Male2 to onto the NanoNevel table.

"Now," Dr. Linden explained, "Let's try out the NanoNevel."

"What is that?" Female1 asked.

Dr. Linden, now adopting a tone of superiority said, "The NanoNevel is a technique Otto Ma...Um, a technique I perfected. We had to hire a coder to program in tons of subroutines."

"We?" Female1 asked.

"Oh, I used to have an assistant," Dr. Lou Pole Linden explained.

"Used to? Where is he or she now?" Male1 asked.

"Uh," Dr. Linden replied, "He's underwater...with his investments. His investments are underwater and he had...um...he's no longer here."

"Dr. Linden," Female1 persisted, "How is it you came here...to this...um...moment."

"What an absurd question from a lab rat," Dr. Linden blurted out.

"Lab rat?" Male1 objected. "Don't call her that."

"Why not?" Dr. Linden pettily defended. "After all, the Matticks used to call me a lab rat behind my back, thinking I didn't know...that I didn't hear. Insulting!" He smiled. "I made one my own assistant."

Female1 replied softly, "So," she looked at him with narrowing eyes, "When the Twins transferred into power, and the Matticks were displaced, you forced one of the Mattick family to become your assistant? To prove you were in control? That you were not a lab rat?"

"Precisely, Female1," Dr. Linden smiled.

"But," Female1 replied, "The reason we are all homeless is because of the Transfer. Because we workers, who were comfortable, not wealthy... not poor... just focused on our jobs..."

Female1 shook her head and started again, trying to appeal to his sympathies, "Because the Twins made it so we workers could not even afford basics such as regular meals or a roof over our heads." She stepped toward him until her chained restraints stretched to their maximum length with a clang.

Male1 added, "What she's saying, Dr. Linden, is that you've literally chained us up so we cannot leave. The Twins have figuratively chained you up so you cannot leave. They have some hold over you."

Female1 nodded. "Dr. Linden, you have

become the thing you once hated. You were insulted, so now you insult. You were pushed aside, so now you push us around. I'll bet the Twins promised you riches in exchange for your cooperation, just as they did all of us in their early propaganda..."

She looked up at Linden with an earnest expression of understanding, "but they lied to you, as well. And, instead of becoming incensed and outraged... you have adopted the characteristics you despised, justifying their petty thievery."

"Why?" She persisted, "So you don't have to admit that they fooled us all? You have a choice, Dr. Linden. You don't need to mimic the Twins to survive."

Dr. Linden looked at her for a long moment, then at the unconscious form of Male2. Then into the piercing eyes of Male1.

Dr. Linden suddenly found it difficult

to maintain eye contact with Male1 and Female1.

He said flippantly, "If you cannot beat them, then one should join…"

"No, Dr. Linden," Male1 interrupted, "If you can't beat them, then you have to get unorthodox."

"Unorthodox?" Dr. Linden scoffed.

Male1 explained, "We all believed the visual promotions that if we cooperated and supported the Twins, they would increase all our profits. If we could simply have the Twins import what we once manufactured on AromaX soil, we'd have jobs…and all be rich."

Female1 added, "All the AromaX jobs…even my accounting job at the bank… all emplacement opportunities moved out of AromaX into territories where the work was done by slaves or robots."

Male1 interjected, "They said the

robots would open up new jobs…like robot programming and repair, but they just trained other robots to do that so the humans didn't have a chance to make a regular income and worked odd jobs here and there- moving around to where the work was- just to keep alive."

Female1 concluded with, "I get 'business is business' and that decision resulted in huge profits for the Twins. But then my job vanished, and there wasn't another way for me to creditably earn money."

"Maybe you were lazy," Linden sneered.

"Lazy?" Female1 scoffed, "I applied to as many jobs as I could! But isn't there a way for the Twins, and for you, Dr. Linden, to get rich in a win-win scenario? Does it have to be zero-sum where the people are zero and get nothing?"

"Zero-sum, my dear, is the only way to win."

Female1 protested, "Can't we also

enjoy the fruits of our labors? If you treat us as disposable, we won't have loyalty for you."

Linden protested, "But you had your homes. Don't act so smug as if everything was ripped away from you. You willingly gave it up because you enjoy living wild as you do."

Female1 spat, "Unhoused? Homeless? Not always a choice. Sometimes a greedy power hungry ruler decides to just take my stuff."

Male1 aggressively responded, "Housing became expensive fast. For no reason. It was an artificial price jump. Then we learn the Twins was buying it all up and evicting us."

Female1 said, "So how did we keep our homes? People took out loans. Borrowed money to keep the the same level of living they had before the Twins."

Male1 enlightened the topic with, "These were loans none of us could afford. Before the Twins came here, we were able get the funds we needed by saving up for a year or two."

Female1 interjected, "Anybody who had a job earned a minimum amount and if that person worked full time, they could afford a two-bedroom-one bathroom residence and still have enough for food and entertainment."

Male1 overlapped Female1's words with, "Then, new taxes were levied to fund agencies to protect us, but we all saw that money went to buying expensive toys for the Twins."

Female1 added, "Almost any political governance system works if those in power are ethical, compassionate toward the people, making decisions to benefit the masses. Likewise, any governance paradigm disintegrates if the people in power abuse the rules and do anything to get more wealth for themselves, and more power, not caring who they sacrifice or eliminate or who gets in their way. But that causes the people to revolt. Anytime integrity and honor are compromised in the throne-room or boardroom, everyone suffers….including the Twins because they will never know who they can really trust."

Male1 explained, "The people of AromaX thought that by supporting the Twins, we were stepping into a warm bath. None of us could feel the water starting to boil. None of us realized at first that the Twins' message would be the citizens of AromaX would all be heroes if we simply consented to being boiled for their lunch."

Female1 chimed in with, "Dr. Linden, bit by bit we all believed the Twins' propaganda…that they could give us a better life, but it was a lie. They are the ones in the boardroom spending the money I had saved up at the bank. I lost everything. They stole from all of us."

Male1 added, "There are no more Matticks in AromaX to oppose the Twins, but you are here, Dr. Linden."

"I am here?" Lou Pole Linden asked softly as he extracted from his pocket, a key to the restraints, which held his captives chained.

"Why should the Twins," Male1 added, "wield their abuses from the boardroom. Why don't you take AromaX back? The people would respect you as their leader, Dr. Linden, if you showed them how much you loved the people and wanted to protect them."

"But," Dr. Linden said weakly as he looked at the key in his hands, "but, I won't be able to maintain power unless I have my own staff of MagSols."

"What?" Female1 asked surprised.

Dr. Linden grabbed a strap and placed it around the feet of the unconscious Male2 on the NanoNevel table, and locked him in. Then, Dr. Linden ran to the other end of the room and hauled out a six foot long transparent domed shell and placed it over Male2.

It looked as if Male2 was lying in a glass coffin. Dr. Linden raced to connect wires and tubes and put on goggles himself.

After frenzied preparation, breathlessly, Dr. Linden turned to Male1 and Female1, tapping the top of the transparent shell, which encased the unconscious Male2 and said, "Want to see the NanoNevel in action?"

6 CHAPTER 42: (2030) AROMAX: LAB: LOU POLE LINDEN- NANONEVEL IS COOKING

Dr. Lou Pole Linden paced. He had now conducted his experiment, using the NanoNevel, which orchestrated millions of nano-sized microscopic robots to attach artificial muscle fibers to the natural muscle fibers of test subject, Male2. The procedure did not require incisions on the patient because the surgery was done on a scale smaller than epithelial skin cells.

But, now Dr. Lou Pole Linden had to

wait.

The other two test subjects, Male1 and Female1, looked in horror as the NanoNevel cloud descended onto the unconscious Male2.

They knew they were helpless to intervene and halt the NanoNevel procedure.

Feeling defeated, Male1 and Female1 lay on their own cots, now accepting the fate that they would be next.

The high pitched buzz irritated them at first, but then they realized there was nothing they could do to stop the painful ringing in their ears.

Lou Pole Linden was jittery and nervous.

If successful, this experiment could move him up to level 2 in the Twin's organization. Maybe one day, he would even be level 1, but only after he had sufficient MagSols to control and turn against the Twins.

Dr. Lou Pole Linden muttered to himself, "Watson, that fake, had the nerve to tell me I was only a level four or five in the Twin's hierarchy and he was a level 2...but...once I demonstrate the MagSols I've created, I will be level 2 for sure."

The armor!

He raced down the hall to check on the development of the exoskeleton armor being fabricated in the work room. It was crude and clumsy, but it would do. He opened his comm and pressed a button to schedule a meeting with the Twins. It was time to show off.

Lou Pole Linden muttered with disdain, "Watson may fleece the people in the corporate cities. He may think he has been running their scam so long that people now accept it as a way of life. They may feel entitled to the money, but I will have the power of my MagSols. And the Twins will love me!"

Then, he heard a clatter down the hall and dropped his comm with annoyance as he ran back to the room with the NanoNevel and the homeless test subjects.

When he skidded through the doorway, Female1 was screaming, "Dr. Linden. Dr. Linden!"

Dr. Linden was greeted with the sight of Male2 attacking Male1. Female1, still restrained by chains yelled to explain,

"Male2 just got up and seemed so angry that he has been swinging at everything. He broke the restraints and escaped from your NanoNevel coffin."

Lou Pole Linden realized that Male2 was in the process of savagely beating his other test subject.

Female1 barked, "He's going to kill us all. Give me the key to protect your investment. You need Male1 and me! Male2 will destroy us if you don't give me your key!"

Lou Pole Linden tossed the keys to Female1 and ordered her to unlock herself and hide in the workroom down the hall. As Female1 was struggling with the key, Dr. Linden carefully approached the men.

"Male2," Dr. Linden started cautiously, "Male1 is your friend. You don't want to kill him. We are all friends."

Male2 spun around and yelled, "I can't control it, Dr. Linden. I have to kill something!"

"That's good, Male2, and you will get to," Dr. Linden replied, "But I need Male1. I must observe you to see how long your strength will last."

Female1 got her restraints unlocked just as Male2 abandoned the crumpled heap of Male1 and now startled Dr. Linden by approaching him.

Dr. Linden backed up a few steps and then with an authoritative roar, said, "Whoa, boy. Calm Down."

Male2 spat, moving with determination, getting closer to Dr. Linden.

"I'm not a horse. I'm not a dog. I'm not a robot. I don't have to follow your orders, Dooooooctor Lou Pole Liiiiiiinden."

Female1 quietly tip toed to Male1who was still lying on the floor, unlocked his restraints, and then silently worked to revive him from his beating.

"I didn't use a robot because," Dr. Linden tried to explain to Male2, "anybody can hack into a robot. I need you to be my loyal MagSols who cannot be hacked nor mind controlled."

"Loyal?" Male2 seethed.

Lou Pole Linden stuttered, "Yes. We are all a... t... t... team... and I am your master who rules with an iron... um... fist."

"Like this?" Male2 asked as he picked up a desk with one hand and flung it across the room, smashing equipment lined up along the wall.

Lou Pole Linden fumbled in his pocket for his tranquilizer gun, but then realized there were no more tranquilizer cartridges left.

Lou Pole Linden skittered to the back of the lab, past Female1, who was still desperately trying to revive Male1.

When Male1 groaned, Female1, hands shaking, and only in basic hospital patient smocks, unlocked and opened the closet to retrieve the smelly clothes she had with her when she and the other two had accepted the lab job offer from the shelter's volunteer employment placement office.

Frantic, she shot a glance over her shoulder at Dr. Linden and Male2, still intensely focused on each other.

Female1 saw Male1, still stunned, push himself until he was able to sit slumped against the wall. She reached up into a cubby-hole and threw Male1 his clothes, leaving the tattered rags of the now ferociously strong Male2 on the shelf.

Female1, hurrying to put on her own clothes while trying to help Male1 to his feet, gasped, "Dr. Linden said to hide in the workroom while he gets our friend under control."

"Why?" Male1 choked, trying to reply.

"Why what?" Female1 responded with nervous energy as she eased him out the door and into the hallway.

Male1 broke away from her and staggered to the wall in the hallway to brace himself.

Male1 continued, "Why are we waiting for Dr. Linden in the workroom. Why don't we just leave?"

Female1 stuttered, "Well... um... I mean... We can't just leave Male2 here. He came with us in the crate. We have to get him back. He's one of us. Everybody else has forgotten about us, so we better not forget about each other!"

"That linden is power-hungry. He's modeling himself after the Twins. He won't spare us. We have to leave now. The only options we have is to fight or flee."

Female 1 argued, "Male2 fought. We can't just flee. Just as our homes and jobs were ripped from us, Male2's own body is being removed from his control. We are a team. We only leave with Male2. He'd do the same for one of us."

Exhausted, Male1 asked, "you sure about that?"

7 CHAPTER 43: (2032) COURTLY CITY: HIGH SCHOOL: SARAH LISTENS TO VIRGINIA HAMM LESSON PLANS & PROMOTE TAKING SIDE JOBS

Georgia Peach waved at Sarah Paradise as Sarah stepped off the bus and started walking toward the imposing grey concrete High School.

"Our school break definitely was not long enough. One week. Good gracious," Georgia remarked as she walked briskly with Sarah trying to make it in time for the first Administrator's meeting before the morning classes commenced. "I'm glad you introduced me to Library and the darling Mrs. Libris."

"Mrs. Libris can find out anything on any topic," Sarah nodded as she carefully stepped across freshly raked tan sand.

"How do you like our new lawn?" Georgia asked. "They sure got it laid out fast. Seven days. Sand. Much easier to tend. No weeds. No mowing. Admin can get things done when it suits them."

Sarah nodded. "But now we need to get back to teaching, right?"

"And," Georgia reminded, "...get back to me showing up at your place when it's time to forget about the workday and go out."

"But," Sarah smiled, "I've saved up. Look." She unzipped her backpack to let Georgia see the top of her new comm. They rested a moment under the shade of a large tree with grey bark which stood on the sidewalk near the road recently paved for wheeled vehicles.

"You got a comm!" Georgia squealed, "Now I can communicate without having to just show up on your doorstep and knock, hoping you're home."

"Well," Sarah shrugged, "If I'm not at school working, I'm either at the grocery store shopping for ingredients, or at home cooking, preparing lesson plans, or grading."

"Well, I love it when you cook with ingredients," Georgia enthused, "But I'm thrilled I can contact you on a comm!"

"So, don't tell anybody," cautioned Sarah, as they resumed walking.

"I didn't register it with the school, yet. Not sure if the Administrators would confiscate it from me," Sarah confided as they neared the school entrance.

"Oh, are we doing confession time? I should tell you, I came by the school last night out of curiosity," Georgia whispered.

"And? Did you see it?" Sarah asked.

"No. It was easy to get into my classroom. Nothing has changed. What was broken during graduation last June, and right through to last week, is still broken. None of the classrooms even had any trash emptied, but I couldn't peek into the Administrative offices.

"They had one of those electronic barriers set up. You know, like the real estate agents have?"

"Will it be opened this morning?" Sarah asked.

"We will find out what they did with the school funds," Georgia winked, "at the emergency meeting Virginia Hamm called for this morning before class."

Sarah glanced at the large campus clock. "I didn't get a meeting agenda."

"It was marked super urgent."

"You're joking. I thought it would just be the usual 'welcome back. Go to class'. Do you know what this urgent meeting is supposed to be about?"

"You didn't get a notice because you haven't registered your comm, Sarah. I just work here, Sugar, and try to keep a low profile and follow orders," Georgia replied with cheerful sarcasm. "Like all over-privileged teachers in this school. Hurry. We need to be on time for Miss Hamm."

When the two women arrived, out of breath, they noted the construction barrier had been removed. The last remains of the Administrative-vacation-remodeling-project were now being cleared away by contract workers.

Georgia ducked to avoid getting hit by a ladder. Sarah nearly slipped on a tarp.

New construction had begun here six months earlier, but no one had been sure exactly what was being done.

When Sarah and Georgia joined the other teachers, they saw everyone looking up at the Administrative Office ceiling. They were stunned to be greeted by soaring arches and a gigantic skylight surrounded by fresco paintings. Gold accents punctuated the ornate crown moldings and rich wood paneling was everywhere.

In one section, there was a new café complete with machines to make "European" coffees. As they stared, a man in a chef's uniform walked by holding aloft a sheet of freshly baked croissants, shouting, "Hot. Hot. Behind you. Hot."

Then, he disappeared through a new door, above which read "Administrative Staff Only."

Apparently, the Administrators had also installed a kitchen during the break. These Administration-approved remodels were a stark contrast to the current shabby state of student classrooms, which stood outdoors subject to blazing summer heat and freezing winter cold, forlorn, unkempt, far off down the long walkway.

Administrator Virginia Hamm appeared, smiling. She pointed to a café counter on which rested a pitcher of water and paper cups next to a stack of salt covered crackers.

Miss Hamm opened the meeting with, "Thank you for attending this emergency confab before your first class of the day. We wanted to show our appreciation and, as you see, we have provided a continental breakfast for you. Please help yourselves."

Again, Virginia Hamm indicated the crackers and water, but ignored freshly baked foods being created in the kitchen behind the "Administrators Only" door.

Georgia Peach whispered to Sarah Paradise, "Look. All the good food is being served to the Administrators in their new facilities back there."

Sarah nodded but kept her eyes on Virginia Hamm.

One teacher asked, "Are teachers permitted to use that new coffee bar?"

Virginia Hamm patiently smiled, "Oh, I'm sorry. This whole area behind me is for Administrative staff only. We really need to pull together like the family we are and be a bit more strict about the budget this year." She shrugged and added, "Unforeseen expenses were incurred."

Georgia leaned toward Sarah and whispered, "Now I see why you had to lose your student desk-chairs and me, my teaching aids."

Sarah replied, "Show team spirit and support..."

Georgia finished the sentence with "Got to feed those Administrators."

"Humph," Sarah concurred, hoping nobody overheard that. She was now self-conscious about her comm and hoped she had turned it off.

Virginia Hamm then announced, "Please take out your HIBs. I'm going to give each of you your new teaching goals for the year."

All of the teachers took out their Holographic Identification Badges and Virginia walked around smiling and pushing HIB buttons to convey specific goals to each teacher.

After Virginia Hamm transmitted Georgia's instructions, Georgia asked, "Um. Miss Hamm?"

"Yes, Miss Peach?" Virginia Hamm smiled with a pageant-practiced picture-ready grin.

"If you remember, last year you confiscated my teaching aids." Georgia cleared her throat and added, "It says here that I'm to lower the level of math taught to my students. Oh, and this also indicates there won't be a text book this year. Am I reading that correctly?"

"We polled your students over the past months and some reported a negative experience," Virginia Hamm explained.

"Would that be from the students who didn't do any homework?" Georgia asked.

Virginia, still smiling laughed, "Always good to start the new school year with a positive attitude, Miss Peach." Then Virginia Hamm added before moving on, "I know you can tell a better story this year."

"Better story?" Georgia asked.

Stepping backwards one pace, Virginia smiled again at Georgia Peach and advised, "I know you teach about irrational imaginary numbers, so this year come up with a better ending and I'm sure your student surveys results will improve. I know you can encourage creativity."

Georgia started to say, "I teach about both real and...I mean irrational numbers have no repeating patterns, but can be seen on a number line whereas imaginary numbers are..."

"I know, I know," Virginia Hamm waved her hand for Georgia to stop, "but the Administrators think real - or those other - numbers may get boring and a little confusing for the students."

She snapped her fingers as if imbued with a fresh idea, "We want to show the parents that we hear them and will make lessons more engaging. So, your assignment, Miss Peach, is to use more fun imaginary numbers during your story time with the students," as she pointed to the HIB Georgia held and whispered, "As it states in your instructions. Okay?"

"Of course, Miss Hamm," Georgia smiled, then softly murmured to herself, "Number line, not story line...whatever..."

Virginia Hamm stopped in front of Sarah Paradise.

"And this is your newly approved educational curriculum." Virginia Hamm pressed a HIB button then remained and asked, "Any questions, Miss Paradise?"

Sarah smiled, glanced over it briefly and started to shake her head no, when something caught her eye.

Sarah said, "It says this year I'll teach ancient history?"

"Yes," Virginia Hamm smiled. "We think keeping you cross-trained will help make your teaching both nimble and strong as it stretches you."

Sarah asked, "But, what happened to our history teacher?"

Virginia Hamm gave a casual wave, "Oh, we assigned him to teach biology. He needs stretching, too."

Sarah glanced over at both the biology

teacher and the history teacher. Both of their faces were streaked with horror.

Sarah added, "These instructions direct me to open up my classes with discussions about tribes of Israel?"

Virginia smiled and said, "That's right. It will help develop the student's conversational skills. With all these technical gadgets to master, some parents were concerned that their children were not developing social skills."

Sarah clarified, "But it says they need to find the lost tribe of Israel as a classroom activity."

Virginia Hamm giggled, "Hunting for that tribe should keep them busy for a few class sessions, right?"

Trying to find the right words, Sarah suggested, "So, I can teach Genesis:35 or Exodus:1? Are you saying, Miss Hamm, I can compare the tribes listed in Genesis:29 to Numbers:1 and

Revelations: 7 to see why Levi is replaced by Ephraim and Manasseh, Joseph's sons, which actually makes 13 tribes?"

Sarah took a breath and deliberately spoke, "I just want to clarify that I am allowed..."

Sarah sped up her speech as she continued, "to teach the students that in Hosea: 4:17, we see that Ephraim worshiped Idols and was removed from the list of tribes. That when the tribe of Dan became idol worshipers, as described in Judges: 17 and 18, Dan was removed from the list of tribes in the book of Revelation, and replaced by only Manasseh?"

Administrator Virginia Ham squinted her eyes as if she did not quite understand Sarah's words.

Sarah paused for one second then speedily continued to avoid being interrupted, "I'm just double checking, Administrator Hamm, that I can ask the students to discuss the characteristics and choices these men made and how it revealed their integrity or lack thereof. How the decision made by an individual impacted the whole tribe...even future generations. Evaluate consequences of the choices made by the original tribes of Israel to see what lessons we apply in today's world... To thinking about consequences of our own daily decisions. I mean, can we learn from Reuben, Simeon, Levi, Judah, Dan, Naphtali, Gad, Asher, Issachar, Zebulun, Joseph and his sons Ephraim and Manasseh or Joseph's younger brother Benjamin?"

"Oh my!" Virginia Hamm giggled, "That was quite a mouthful. I certainly hope you don't babble like that to your students." She shook her head and indicated Sarah's HIB, "All us Administrators worked very hard on each of the teacher assignments over the last few months. Watson is such an inspirational leader."

Sarah said, "I'm just trying to understand this history assignment, Miss Hamm."

Virginia Hamm stopped smiling and ordered, "Read aloud what your HIB says for your assigned teaching curriculum, Miss Paradise. Word for word."

Sarah hesitated, embarrassed, then cleared her throat and read as instructed, "The ancient history teacher will create a fun activity to help students find the lost tribe of Canine."

"That's right, Miss Paradise. It is not difficult to understand. Your job is to create a game so the students eventually find the lost tribes of Canine by the end of the school year...in your classroom."

"Really? The lost tribes of Canine?" To clarify, Sarah spelled, "C-a- n-i-n-e?"

Miss Hamm gave a curt nod. "Just as it instructs you on your HIB. This is a better way for students to have a solid year of ancient history and respond to the parent's wish for their children to be well rounded. That is why we created that assignment."

Sarah asked, "Do the Administrators mean the ancient geographic region of Canaan, named for the grandson of Noah, as in Genesis: 10? Or Canine, Miss Hamm? As in...a group of dogs..."

Virginia Hamm shook her head "I have other teachers to deliver goals to, Miss Paradise. I can't do your job and mine. Just make learning fun."

Sarah nodded realizing any reasoning was futile, "Yes, Miss Hamm."

Hamm gathered herself ready to exit and then turned to impart one last pearl of wisdom for Sarah by adding, "Show them a visual of puppies and teach the students to fetch a treat...How hard is it to find a visual of a pack of dogs, Miss Paradise. I mean really...teach them about how to find canine, lost land of dogs."

"Maybe I could use a map..." Sarah offered.

Miss Hamm laughed to herself as she

finished her thought, "I mean obviously we wouldn't have dogs- as pets today if they were really lost..."

"I'll start preparations for the class, as you advise, Miss Hamm."

"Remember only use school approved texts and lesson plans. The Administrators made it so easy for all you teachers. All you need to do is follow the instructions. You do not need any extra props like...maps. I just sent you the lesson plan. Follow it. The Administrators work hard to do all the thinking for you teachers, Miss Paradise."

Sarah nodded politely and said, "Yes, Miss Hamm. I know the Administrators worked very hard on ... These are indeed very clear teacher instructions. Dogs. Lost canines. Yup. Thank you."

Then, smiling brightly, Virginia Hamm announced to the group, "This is a reminder that as of this year, for each holiday break, you will not get paid. This applies to all teachers. You are welcomed, however, to get a side job as long as it doesn't interfere with your teaching goals."

Virginia Hamm moved along to the next perplexed teacher, dismissing the instructors who had already received their lesson plan uploads to their HIBs so they could begin their new assignments.

8 CHAPTER 44: (2032) COURTLY CITY: HIGH SCHOOL: GEORGIA INFORMS SARAH, MR. ELEMENT'S STRAWBERRIES & THE PARTY:

"Can you believe it?" Georgia Peach, frustrated teacher, stormed into Sarah's classroom just as Sarah's students were leaving for the day. Georgia waited for the last student to exit before she twisted her face into a mask of angry disapproval.

Without another word, Georgia grabbed Sarah's arm and tugged her to follow, obviously too upset to even speak. She marched Sarah outdoors to the back of the school and showed her a plot of land.

The warm tan sand blended into a square patch of dark, espresso- bean brown, rich loose earth.

"Look at that!" Georgia demanded pointing to the soil while beckoning another teacher, Mr. Element, to join them.

Georgia Peach turned to Mr. Element and said, "Tell her. Tell Miss Paradise, here, what our beloved administrator Miss Virginia Hamm just told you."

Mr. Element shrugged, "Um," he started, "As you know, I used to be the life science teacher, but am now assigned to Courtly Corporation history."

He looked sadly at dark green leafy clumps which had begun to spring out of the black soil. Tiny strawberries peeked from their umbrellas of mature dark green leaves.

"Yes?" Sarah Paradise prompted, "I've been assigned to ancient history of religions, I think."

"Well," Mr. Element continued, "I suppose I could ask my students about the difference between mitosis of a cell and meiosis."

Sarah replied, "Mitosis is used by single cell organisms to reproduce. When a cell divides, it results in two genetically identical cells. Meiosis is the division of a germ cell, which will contain half the number of chromosomes of the original cell."

Mr. Element shrugged, "Fine. That's basic biology. But I'm a chemist. I instruct bright, High School chemistry students. My concentration has always been chemistry. Not gardening and not history."

Georgia Peach put a gentle hand on Mr. Element's shoulder. "Do you see what I mean? Miss Paradise knows things."

Sarah shook her head, "Honestly, I just remember that Mitosis has two 'I's which are mirror images, so splitting will have the same number of chromosomes.

Meiosis starts with 'me' as in 'eeeeech', so must be an icky germ cell and only want half of those chromosomes. What is all this about?" Sarah asked.

"What Miss Peach is trying to say," Mr. Element started, "is that although I should teach chemistry, Administrator Hamm has assigned me to teach Courtly history. Oddly, she seems to think that means my teaching goal is to show the students how to grow fruits and vegetables."

Sarah Paradise asked, "Mr. Element, how does growing veggies tie in with the history of Courtly City?"

Mr. Element shrugged, "Something about honoring the Earth Farmer subculture."

"Pardon me?" Sarah asked.

Mr. Element shrugged. "I do not know. Maybe... Growing strawberries...um...I guess is a symbol for when the Earth Farmers settled around here. I don't have a problem with shoving a seed in the ground, Miss Paradise, except the plants seem to get devoured by pill bugs or slugs. I don't know what to do. I have to grow something to show the Administrators. Miss Peach here thought you'd be able to help me figure something out."

"About your assignment?" Sarah asked.

"Yes," Georgia pleaded, "If Mr. Element can't grow his strawberries, he will get a negative review by the end of the year and could lose his job. You can sympathize with that, can't you? You cook with ingredients, so I figured, you'd know how to grow those ingredients, as well."

Sarah paused. "Well, I know teachers need to stick together." She looked up and continued, "And I seem to remember learning some basics about gardening when I was younger, but..."

Sarah knelt down to examine the small rows of plants. It appeared that Mr.

Element was trying to grow strawberries but each berry was covered in pill bugs, who were happily eating away at the fruit.

Georgia persisted, "Every teaching goal assignment has to be presented when the Administrators have their cocktail soirée. Administrator Virginia Hamm is going to have a practice party so she can impress her bosses with how happy we are."

"Cocktail soirée?" Sarah asked, "Practice party?"

Mr. Element stepped in, "Oh, I guess you didn't read the new notice Administrator Hamm sent out."

"Notice about what, Mr. Element?"

Mr. Element explained, "Virginia Hamm does not have the budget for student supplies, but she does have the budget for her practice party. Attendance is after hours and mandatory. Miss Hamm says she wants to try out various food and beverage options to set the appropriate tone for the night the executive administrators come to our school."

Georgia added with a roll of her eyes, "She wants to make sure we all behave properly so she can showcase our fabulous work to her management."

Sarah asked, "When is this party?"

Georgia replied, "First one is tonight." She smiled, "Did your students find where in your classroom you stashed the lost tribe of canine, yet?"

9 What Just Happened?

Sarah is dealing with the internal struggle to share the truth with her students, to fact check her lesson plans with the demands of the Administrators who do not care about the facts, and are forcing Sarah to use her position of teacher to share with the students either false data or information which does not really encourage student critical thinking. Instead the administrators want Sarah to entertain.

Meanwhile, Female1 and Male1 tried to appeal to Dr. Linden by explaining the plight of the people. These "lab rats" tried to appeal to his ego to be the leader and stand up to the Twins. Dr. Linden, instead, see the Twins as a way of getting his own wealth and power faster. Even though he has seen the Twins betray and lie to the people, Dr. Linden thinks he is the exception and will not be lied to.

The lesson Sarah struggles with is choosing between teaching true facts and actively discussing how our choices do matter and impact those around us versus presenting entertainment... So the students are passively engaged, which is what the Administration wants. The administrators seem to discourage critical thinking and wish for a docile, compliant student citizen who will never question anything. Will Sarah do what is true, or what she is ordered to do?

The lesson form the AromaX Lab is that any organization can be corrupt if a person in power makes decisions to only benefit themselves at the expense of those around them. This would justify lying and harming people as if they were disposable and interchangeable. This also means the leader is never able to trust his subjects, and because of that will constantly demand "tests of loyalty" to prove the leader can still give the most bizarre of orders and have them followed without question. The consequence of this is that the people may engage in rebellion and revolt because 'rule is always zero-sum', meaning one person must lose and one must win, instead of win-win, which means all parties get something they want and can co-exist.

10 Did You Know...

The term NanoNevel is created for this story to summarize a process whereby a MagSol, or enhanced super magnificent soldier, could be created. The term NanoNevel is from "Nano" or "nanotechnology", which is a type of technology which focuses on very small elements, usually with dimensions of less than 100 nanometers.

This means that individual molecules and atoms can be manipulated.

The term *Nevel*, is taken from two places. First, it can be used as a verb to describe an act of beating with fists or pounding or pummeling. It was used by John Knox (c1514–1572), religious reformer.

Some use the term to mean to grip with fingers or to knead or squeeze with fingers.

In Dutch it means a fog or haze.

So this term, NanoNevel, is used in this story to describe the procedure Dr. Linden uses.

In his lab at AromaX, Dr. Linden's NanoNevel manipulates small molecular sized elements infused with artificial intelligence.

This mixture acts as a descending fog or haze which can be directed with a program.

The haze or fog lowers onto a patient, such as Male2. The tiny nano-sized robots will collectively knead or pummel Male2's skeletal structure electrochemically with these nano-structures to interlace his own natural muscle fibers with artificial muscle fibers. The artificial muscle fibers are nano-composite fibers, which can lift about 1,000 times or more than a non-enhanced muscle fiber.

Research is ongoing to constantly improve artificial muscle by making it cheaper, more responsive and stronger.

These can be used to help people with muscle deficiency, but it can also be used in a variety of other applications. Some speculate that enhancing the muscles of a normal human would give them super-human strength. Others surmise this procedure should only be used on those with diminished muscles so that they could regain the strength of a normal average human.

10 Vocabulary

This fictional series introduces some words unique to this world. Also used are standard terms which we encourage you to investigate in a dictionary for your own edification. A consolidated full list of vocabulary for all GONE books is located in the Conversation Station supplemental book.

Onsie   Usually a garment worn by a toddler to include a single unit of clothing which covers legs, arms and torso and, often, feet.

NanoNevel   Term used in this story to define the fog or haze (borrowed from the

Dutch language) of nanotechnology which is used during an operation

NanoNevel manipulates small molecular sized elements infused with artificial intelligence to act as a fog or haze which will descend on a patient and knead or pummel his skeletal structure electrochemically with these nano-structures to interlace the patients own natural muscle fibers with artificial muscle fibers, which are nano-composite artificial fibers which can lift about 1,000 times or more their weight.

Unorthodox Something not usually done

HIB Holographic Identification Badge. In Courtly City, the HIB uses your profession and then your name instead of a Mr. or a Mrs. so the title would be Teacher Sarah Paradise, Reporter Bjorn Esterday, Administrator Virginia Hamm. The HIB can contain your train ticket. The HIB also conveys instructions for your job, as Miss Hamm gave Miss

Paradise her lesson plan instructions.

Aerogel   Carbon aerogel epoxy polymer composite can act as a shield against hot and cold

gigapascals,   A unit or pressure equal to 10^9 pascals. Geophysicists use the gigapascal (GPa) in measuring or calculating tectonic stresses and pressures.   A unit of pressure can quantify internal pressure, stress, and ultimate tensile strength.
Aggregated diamonds have an isothermal bulk modulus of 491 gigapascals, which is stronger than carbon diamonds

Aggregated diamond   Aggregated diamond nanorods (ADNRs) are a nanocrystalline form of diamond (nanodiamond or hyperdiamond). A diamond is carbon with atoms arranged in a crystal formation (Diamond cubic). Some very strong diamonds can only be scratched by other diamonds and nanocrystalline diamond aggregate. In the story, Dr. Lou Pole Linden reads, "...Kevlar net against the fullerene carbon- hydrogen nano-structures amorphous diamond film until still pliable. Then shape against desired mold."

Administrators   These are select people in the education field in Courtly City who structure precisely what each teacher will teach. In this story, Administrator Virgina Hamm gives Sarah Paradise instructions for her classroom via Sarah;s HIB.

Lexan   A transparent plastic (polycarbonate) of high impact strength, used for windscreens in airplane or jet cockpit canopies, bulletproof screens, etc. It is clear enough to see out of like a window, but also very strong.

Transparent Alumina   (aluminum oxynitride or AION)   This is a transparent polycrystalline ceramic material which mixes aluminum, nitrogen, and oxygen so that you can still see through it in the near-ultraviolet, visible, and infrared light regions. This can be strong enough to withstand shots from small caliber weapons.

Mailable Inspector Collector This term is the title of an invention patented in 2021 at the USPTO or United States Patent and Trademark Office. Patent number 11,077,436.

It was created in response to the COVID19 pandemic. This invention was "fast tracked" because it was one of a limited number of patent applications which proved it would benefit the general public and meet other regulatory requirements.

The invention's purpose was to support early pathogen (virus or bacteria) detection in geographies which did not have access to sophisticated laboratory equipment, yet needed to know if the lingering virus was in the environment.

The design considered bio-degradable easy-to-access stock supplies to make manufacturing easy.

The design also included a process of mass-distribution and recycling for environmentally friendly disposal. It leveraged existing infrastructure for delivery, such as the United States

Postal Service or other courier service. This supply-chain process was included in the design to minimize trash, litter, and other waste. When manufactured commercially, it may have a different name.

ABOUT Wynter Sommers

Wynter Sommers is the pseudonym for an American writing team, which harnesses multiple skills in technology, research, history and education. Formally trained with a PhD in Education, Wynter Sommers blends academic classroom experience, with corporate sophistication, and a passion for developing more effective student insights through engaging storytelling.

Wynter Sommers has a heart to inspire creativity and develop critical thinking skills, all to encourage readers to make wise choices in life.

Wynter Sommers takes each story and weaves the plot with classic gripping elements, which endure throughout repeated readings, revealing new meanings each time the story is explored. The small choices a reader makes in real life could have a lasting effect in future generations. This set of stories shows the origin of not just Bjorn Esterday and Sarah Paradise, but of their ancestors and the sort of world which was established, which unfolded in each generation until Bjorn and Sarah met.

It is rewarding to learn of heartfelt, thought provoking conversations taking place globally about the characters of these books. Should the reader be presented with extraordinary circumstances, it is the sincerest wish that they act with honor, truth and integrity to overcome obstacles in real life whilst the reader hones skills of self-reliance and collaborative teamwork despite barriers outside of the reader's control. Wynter Sommers hopes you enjoy the other ***Bjorn Esterday Was not Born Yesterday*** stories in this series.